I0822325

EXODUS-B

Exodus-b

MORGAN PLANTZ

made Baugh us

Made Baugh Us

This book is dedicated to my beloved Timothy Baugh, and our four children: Archer, Luna, Leon, and Ruby. May your dreams come true no matter what age you are. I love you all so much and thank you for believing in me. I will forever cherish you.

Love, Momma

Note Before Reading
From the Author

While this book is entirely fiction, I am not writing this to change your thoughts on what Earth is for or any religion that you follow. The beauty of the world is that you have the right to believe in any religion you want to. I had an epiphany one day that got me thinking about what the Earth and the universe were really about. I do not plan to sway you into thinking that is wild and outlandish. I just thought it would make a good story. For those that believe in certain religions, please do not think I am blaspheming your God. In fact, I believe I am expanding on the thought processes of thousands of years of certain beliefs.

This story focuses on a woman that had been through so many hard times and wanted to know what lies beyond. We have *no* idea what happens beyond the grave. We have our books and our teachings from years before us. Our family's ideas, and those of our friends. To know what happens is to be dead. To be dead is the end. Or is it?

Enjoy the ideals of this story, and don't automatically assume I am trying to destroy faith. That is the *last* thing I am doing. This is a fictional, sci/fi story that holds no grounds for anything. I thoroughly enjoyed researching the unknown of Proxima Centauri and the surrounding areas for this book. I hope you enjoy the characters inside of this fantasy world.

~ 1 ~

Chapter 1
Heaven and Hell

I heard death was the end of growing up. Once you die, you're sent off into the abyss. Into darkness. If you didn't believe in God, you went to hell. But the only thing of hell I heard was fire and constant pain. The Lord said to ask for forgiveness, no matter what you did wrong. Ask for forgiveness and you will be forgiven. Forgiveness equals Heaven. So technically speaking, you could murder and rape and beat and do all the things against the 10 commandments, and if you say "Lord, please forgive me," you are exonerated and go to Heaven.

This was the way I was brought up in this world since I was 5. I went to a protestant church my whole life. What is a protestant? To this day, I still am not sure what a protestant church is compared to a "normal" Christian church. According to Dr. Google, *a protestant is a member or follower of any of the Western Christian churches that are separate from the Roman Catholic Church and follow the principles of the Reformation, including the Baptist, Presbyterian, and Lutheran churches.* Do you understand this? I didn't.

I was now 47 years old. I hadn't stepped foot in a religious building since I was 28, the day I decided there was more to the afterlife than heaven and hell. If the Earth is magnificent and beautiful, but somehow has wildfires, tornados, and hurricanes that destroy its exquisiteness, how does it sustain millions of lives? What is the point of living if you're just going to die? There are people starving in Africa and other third-world countries. The kids are filled with worms and eat a meal once every seven days if you can call it a meal. Their parents try their best to kill an animal to feed their family, but they are out there hunting lions, boars, and wild dogs. There are no police. There is murder and cannibalism happening every day just to survive. What is their purpose on this planet?

Wars have ravaged Iraq, Afghanistan, and Ukraine. A nuclear warhead destroyed Chernobyl. Even Hiroshima got obliterated by an atomic bomb. Cancer has consumed first responders since 9/11/2001. Worldwide devastation has amassed every corner of the world. And yet, we wake up every morning, get dressed for work, drink our coffee, argue with our spouses, lie with our mistresses, and relish the lives we live.

After every rainfall, there's a rainbow. After a volcano erupts, new land is constructed. A massive wildfire sparks, and yet new trees sprout from the ground like the foundation has just been germinated. Exquisite flowers, enormous Sequoia trees, and plains thousands of miles long engulf the surface of this world. Beauty and pain, pain and beauty. It all goes hand in hand. You can't have success without suffering. The coastal lines are filled with tranquility. Hell, humpback whales have even taught themselves to catch krill in Antarctica by blowing bubbles in alluring patterns that don't happen anywhere else in the world. Heaven and Hell coexist on the same expanse. We must find clarity.

Chapter 2
Hypochondriac

I awoke this morning feeling peculiar. There was a fluttering in my chest that felt as though someone was blowing bubbles through a straw in my heart. I had always had weird aches and pains throughout my life. My husband of ten years had without fail gotten angry due to always having something wrong with my body. I was perceived to have suffered from hypochondria, but my pain was always real. I started my Mr. Coffee with Colombian coffee beans that I made every morning. I took my exceptionally hot shower that felt as though I burned 7 layers of dead skin off every time. The bubbling never subsided. My heart was racing but I didn't want to wake up my very grumpy spouse to let him know something else was inevitably wrong with my ever-failing body.

I poured my coffee into my to-go mug that had a decal on the side that stated *I tried,* making fun of my inability to talk to people in the mornings before my java hit my nervous system and cooled my morning bitchiness. Crawling into my Hummer H3 that my dear husband bought me for my birthday one year, I sneezed and subsequently spilled my coffee *everywhere.* My leather seats were saturated, and my white knickers were now stained brown. I was running late for my meeting that I could not miss, so I said *fuck it* and left.

Driving down i-75 was a nightmare. Between constant construction and dumbasses crashing because they were staring into the meta world, forgetting the "real" world is a thing. They were thinking only of the inconsistent squirrels running rampant and wild in their fast-driven and electronically dopamine-filled minds.

I looked down at my watch, succumbing to the will of the binding word called time...I was going to be late now! One car after another passed me at a time faster than my own, with lives too busy to care enough about cutting in front of me and my timeline. I muttered a curse under my breath as another one of those mindless robots texting on their phone jumped in front of me only to hit the brakes to get off the exit. The race was on to be just one more car length ahead before exiting to their more important life, or so they thought.

There were many reasons why I chose not to be on the major interstates and that was only one of the many happening here. I felt a tightening in my chest and my breath faltered as I was grasping for control in this devilish contest for recognition in this particle of a world in a vast universe. My eyes started to blur, and I saw static and heard a weird noise in my head like an old record player on high speed.

I clenched the armrest beside me to try and regain a hold onto reality as I slipped into a world of pain and discomfort starting from my chest on down through my arms and into my whole being. Morbid thoughts started running through my head. "I am going to die," I thought.

I could hear my husband's annoyed voice telling me I was fine and just having another childish fit. Then I drifted to thoughts of my family and wondered if they would miss me as I started to lose consciousness.

BEEP! A semi truck's horn blared out as I was swerving over into the other lane, waking me out of whatever condition I was in, bringing me back to reality for a slight second before I saw the divider wall crashing into me, or was I crashing into it? Then blackness.

Chapter 3
The Great Divide

I woke up with a ringing in my ears and a bright light flashing in my eyes. Wait! It wasn't flashing, it was more of a constant thrumming in my eyes as well as my ears. I reached over to my phone to have something of mine that I kept close, so I could regain a hold onto what just happened, but I couldn't *feel* anything...I could only hear and see that fluctuating bright light, and I was starting to get annoyed. And then, I became very calm.

My senses became aware and I could smell different aromas, yet I could not smell at all. I could feel everything around me, yet I could not feel at all. My hearing was impeccable, but I had always had trouble with my hearing. My breath was smooth, yet I was not breathing. My eyes started to focus on the bright light, and all clarity became known to me. I was dead...

I was ECSTATIC!! I've always wanted to be dead! I even daydreamed about it, wishing I could blow my brains out. Joking about it, but in reality, being serious. This was going to be great! I had nobody to be disappointed in me and nobody to worry about now because they were stuck in that cesspool of a human body and earth. I was somewhere amazing and different. Everything my heart desired was here, and I could relish and enjoy EVERY moment of this form from now on.

I had awakened into a place where I felt was so familiar, yet I had never been there. I knew this place. I was... Love. I was living now, in love! My worries were not there. My pain? Gone. My thoughts? I knew, so I just did. How could I explain this to anyone I ever knew? No words could express or even touch the realm of what type of reality this was. In an instant, I knew quantum theory. I understood the many attributes and *methods* of physics, yet humanity hadn't grasped the concept that there were no “rules” as they put it. There was the known and the unknown, and I knew!

I wanted to jump up and down for joy but my motions were constricted in a way that was familiar, yet I could not completely see the outcome of this particular situation I found myself in. I felt as though my whole body was wet and warm. My entire existence was floating in the darkness, but there was a light at the end of the tunnel. I was able to hear a voice outside of where I was, and everything that was said burned a hole through my brain, staying there. It was like burning information onto a floppy disk.

I started to reflect on my life. What had I done in the 47 years I had lived? The average person would've had children and a career. I barely graduated high school. I was the kid who squeezed by with D's and C's all throughout school because I didn't give a shit. I just wanted to graduate so I could move out of my parent's house and start my life. When you turn 18 you're an adult, right? I, in fact, did move out, but ended up in a crappy apartment, in a crappy town working for the local fast food restaurant that didn't even pay me enough for my rent.

I had a boyfriend that was nine years older than me at eighteen. He was a bad boy that sold drugs on the local corner. I tried it one time, a pill. I don't remember what kind it was, but it made me go literally psycho and scared the shit out of me, so I never touched it again. I was going nowhere fast with this guy.

Chapter 4
Letting Bygones be Bygones

Fast forward seven years, and I finally left him after he blackened my face. He had had too much booze and I put ketchup and mustard on only one side of his burger bun instead of both sides. He threw the bun into the wall and made it stick, then swung around and cold-cocked me right in the cheekbone. I passed out and plopped onto the floor. The second I awoke, I was out the door. I left my apartment and *all* of my belongings. I took the clothes on my back and my beaten down car on its last leg.

I found a job as a secretary at a law firm with which I had *zero* experience. I gave them my sob story and they gave me a shot. I had been at that inferior job with minimum wage ever since. That was where I met my husband. He was a player who always told me he was dating to find someone to marry again, but that ended up being hundreds of women before and during me. I didn't realize at the time that he was a narcissist, but it turned out he was the most narcissistic of all. I was making a small amount of *coin* to pay for my tiny apartment. I was skinny and beautiful and I knew I could make a living on my own, but he got a hold of me somehow. Whether it was his sweet charm and his *good morning darling* text messages he'd sent me every morning, I didn't know what actually made me say *this is the one.*

The little jabs at me started a week into the relationship if you could call it that at the time. Little things would make him angry at me. If I forgot to do something as small as making a call to the local grocery store to see if they had a certain item that he didn't necessarily need at the time. If I hadn't gotten his laundry done the day he took them off, even though it wasn't my job and I wasn't living with him. If his house was a mess from him coming home from work and me not putting away his cooler even though I wasn't living with him. I was supposed to go to his house and make sure everything was done. Even feeding his cats, I had to make sure it was done even though they weren't mine yet.

It slowly progressed into me not reminding him of *his* bills needing to be paid when I didn't open his mail. It was not my responsibility to remind him yet. I was trying to make my minuscule living by myself but somehow ended up intertwined with his. He always *toned* me over it. I was never allowed to say he yelled at me because it would make him seem like the bad guy, which he could never be. He knew I didn't have a lot of money and was just scraping by.

One day, my druggy ex showed up out of the blue and corralled me into a corner. I wanted nothing to do with him, but he wanted to show me that he was still there. He forced himself onto me over my dining room table right before I was going to meet my now-husband. I tried to fight back but he was tall, heavyset, and mean. He overpowered me. I couldn't stop the rape. I tried. I kicked him and pushed him but I was so small and insignificant that he just took all of my willpower. I finally got him off after, and I ran out of the door. I cried and I cried. I told my now-husband about it when I got to the parking lot of the grocery store where I was meeting him. He could tell I was upset but the whole situation pissed him off even more. He told me it was *my* fault that I had been raped. I had a gun a whole flight of stairs away from me and he thought I should have been able to shove the very obese man off of me, run up my stairs, find my key to my gun safe, and run *back* down the stairs to shoot the man that was raping me. It would have never worked out that way.

From that moment forward, my now-husband stated that he couldn't trust me. I couldn't defend myself from a man. That made him look at me like I was a fly on a wall. There was no reason for me to be there and I couldn't defend myself from a simple fly-swatter. In reality, I tried so hard to get him off of me but he was just too big. I had hated myself ever since that day. My now husband never forgave me for that day. He constantly brought it up in arguments. He got to the point where he was seeing other people because he couldn't trust me even though *I* was the one who was raped. He would date a woman for a few weeks to a month and he would see me in the meantime. He told me he loved me every day, would leave the person he was dating to spend time with me, but wouldn't commit to me.

This went on for years. It broke me more than you could ever imagine. I tried to date in the meantime but he would always find out and he would ruin the relationships I had made. He would constantly berate me while I was with another person even though he was with another at the same time in the room. He demolished everything. He would always apologize to me after and make me feel like he loved me and that the other girls meant nothing to him. I was young and dumb and naive. I thought he loved me even after all the bullshit.

On my birthday one year though, he bought me my Hummer. He had a white one of his own and he told me this was him *choosing* me. He said it was going to be in my name and I would finally have something that was *mine.* He officially moved me into his home and said *mi casa su casa* basically what's mine is yours. I thought we had finally become one. Boy, was I wrong.

As the years progressed, he developed an even worse gambling addiction than he had before. He had a ton of money when he met me, but he wanted something more. He wanted a big barndominium for us to raise a family in. Albeit, he didn't have enough for it, so he started messing with stocks, gambling centers, and lottery tickets. No matter how much I asked him not to spend thousands of dollars on these things, he stated he needed to so that he could make a life for us and our future children.

This habit turned into thousands of dollars being wasted on gambling items that never amounted to *anything.* Thousands of dollars turned into twenty-six thousand dollars being owed to the IRS along with fifty thousand dollars indebted to credit card companies because he would take out multiple credit card loans, so he could gamble them into the stock market to maybe or maybe not make money. Somehow, even though I *always* told him to stop spending money on stuff that wouldn't get us anywhere, he still did it. And it was still *my* fault always.

I came across an article one day about a narcissist. I had heard the word before but never really knew what it meant. As I read, I stopped dead in my interweb of tracks. This made total sense. He was as narcissistic as narcissists get. Though it didn't change anything, at least I knew then why he was the way he was. His mother had always told me he was different but didn't think of him as a bad person. My in-laws were very religious and thought the world of their son, even though they knew he wasn't perfect. They wanted to believe he was holy. They didn't know about the anger, and the hurt he preyed upon people. They didn't know about the words he spewed from his sweet-loving jaws.

Every time he came through the front door or woke up from a nap, he would make sure to bring up a situation that he expected me to take care of even though it wasn't my problem. It was almost like he purposefully did it just to start an argument. He always knew the things I wouldn't take care of due to no fault of my own. I didn't have the best memory from a prior health condition that involved a lot of magnesium sulfate to keep me from going into a seizure, and he knew that. He used it to his advantage to make a scene.

Years of this abuse, even if it was only emotional, took a toll on my small body. I started gaining weight that I hadn't ever done in my life. He made me think something was wrong with my brain to where I started taking antidepressant medication so he couldn't blame an argument on me being *insane.* Those pills actually caused me to have depression and anxiety and messed me up way more than I had been before. Though even after I started taking them, the arguments turned to *oh, did you take your pill,* or you're *acting like this because you're psycho because you're on medication.* Technically, it made everything worse. And it really ended up screwing up my emotions more per the side effects. I subsequently had to stop taking the medication due to the off-shoot of side effects, but that didn't solve the problem. It made it worse. He proceeded to blame all of our problems on stopping the meds. I couldn't ever get ahead.

Chapter 5
Reborn

The light I saw as I opened my eyes proceeded to dim the more I blinked. I tried to focus on what was in front of me, but for some reason, I couldn't. I raised my hand in front of my face. What the hell?! Why the hell do I have a baby hand?! I went to scream and all I heard was an infantile cry. This can *not* be real. I closed my eyes hoping and praying that I would wake up from this nightmare. Warmth wrapped around my body. A blanket? No, hands. Hands were wrapped around me lifting me from the hard surface I was supposedly laying on. An angelic voice rang through my senses, and a calmness followed. I stopped crying and looked to see who or what was pressing against my flesh.

The face I saw was familiar. I knew this person. She started to speak and I could hear her words but I could not see her mouth move.

***

"Hello, my sweet child. Oh, have I waited so long for you," the person said.

***

Was this telepathy? I was in awe. I knew things I never knew before. Things that were so advanced for our civilization, and yet I didn't know why.

***

"Stand up my dear," the lady vocalized to me in her brain. "I realize this is so very strange to you, but trust me, for I am your mother."

***

This woman standing in front of me *did* look like my mother. Though my mother was dead. She had passed when I was dating my first abusive boyfriend. He had taken me from all of my family. I couldn't even go to the funeral or reception. I had found out through the grapevine, but the bastard wouldn't let me call my grieving siblings.

***

"Up, up, little one. I will explain everything in time. I forgive you for the funeral, my love," my mother spoke softly.

***

Again, what the hell. I didn't know how many more times I could say it.

***

"On this plane, little one, we don't curse. Cursing, we have learned, facilitates anger. There is no anger here," she explained without speaking.

***

A world without anger, I thought to myself. What would a world without anger be like? It's unfathomable. That would never happen. All the screwed-up stuff. Wait, no, all the things wrong and evil that have happened on Earth in the hundreds of years, were all caused by anger. Also, why did she keep telling me to stand up? I was just a few minutes old. My mother emphasized *on this plane*, whatever that means, they have learned to communicate through thoughts. Everyone on the plane could hear every single person's thinking and knew what their actions were going to be next.

I focused very hard on my little tiny legs and begged them to stand. My mother wrapped her hands under my armpits and gently raised me to a standing position.

***

"Let your legs catch your weight, I won't let you fall. Trust me." Her voice was so soothing.

***

I let my mass fall into my little legs. I was scared, but I had known my mother my whole life, and I knew she wouldn't let me falter. She held me while I caught my bearings *and then she let go!* I shrieked for a moment before realizing I was standing by myself.

How was this possible? She grabbed my hand and whispered *run* through my mind.

I took off at speeds I couldn't believe. Even with how small I was, I was so quick. The feeling of the grass spread through my toes, and it was *bliss*. The grass literally felt like one giant chinchilla blanketed the ground.

***

"My child, welcome to Centauri-b," her voice rang through my head.

***

Chapter 6
The Plane of Ecstasy

Looking around while I was galavanting through the fields with my mother, all I saw was green. Huge, beautiful trees. Grass for as far as your eyes could see. Animals filled the land, every one of them coexisting with each other. As far as I could tell, I didn't see any other people. Wait, what was that that I was hearing? Or thinking? This was still so confusing. I paused for a second. I was hearing the animals conversing with each other. At that moment, I felt my mother's hand squeeze mine. I looked up, and she smiled the biggest grin and nodded.

She took me through the fields of grazing gazelle, past the sun-bathing crocodiles, stopping to pet the African Wild Dogs that were weaving through. This was astounding. We trekked long miles, and yet I never tired.

***

"I have heard of Centauri-b, but the scientists on Earth could never see close enough to get any more information other than it was possibly inhabitable, but it was rocky and irradiated," I thought to her.

***

She giggled before explaining in her thoughts that the radiation produced a front that made the world look rocky and unwelcoming, so that life on Earth wouldn't try to develop a way to fly through space and outside the galaxy to get there. She spoke about how this world was the next level of life. The purpose of Centauri-b was to foster those souls that found their purpose on Earth. Those that had hate in their hearts originally, had learned to love. The ones that were meant to teach, taught.

Some people learned at a very early age, and for some, it took until eighty-plus years to finally understand why they were meant to be on Earth. That's why twenty-year-olds stopped breathing. Babies that passed had a much larger purpose. The folks that lived for more than a century were the ones that needed to help the young figure out how to find themselves. People weren't meant to be on Planet Earth forever. Earth was for learning. Earth was for being. Earth was for dying again.

***

"That is a conversation for another time, though. I want to take you to meet your family that found their objective on Earth before you. Everyone you ever knew that has died, is here," she explained to me.

***

We walked through a line of trees that opened into a vast prairie. There were small huts, made of what looked like clay, with straw for a roof. It reminded me of the old adobe houses we learned of in school. There were no roads. There were no skyscrapers. What I did see that resembled *technology were* wind turbines and solar panels connected to each house.

***

"Everything here is powered by our sun and our streams," my mother replied to my thoughts.

***

A world that is untouched by humanity's greed. Needing to *develop* a country that literally destroys the grasslands and great forests that used to blossom on Earth. This was the most beautiful place I had ever hoped to see. Who knew that time would be on a different planet than the one I had known for forty-seven years.

As we walked closer to the huts, a mass of people gathered around my mother and me. People of all ages. I heard their voices all at the same time, and yet somehow I could make out what each person was thinking to me. It was loud and organized simultaneously. Everyone hugged me and I knew who each person was. Even family members that had died before I was born *the first time* but I had known them through the family tree and all of the pictures I had been shown throughout my life. This was where they all rested.

A woman came forward through the thicket of my family. She had snow-white hair and smelled of roses. There was a slight aroma of bengay, that cream that the elderly wore for their arthritis. It was my great-grandma. I had only known her for a short time in my previous life, but she was always in my corner. Her love was unyielding for me. I ran to her and gave her a big bear hug on her leg. I was still this tiny baby walking around on my little legs, but I used all of my might to show my appreciation for seeing her again. She had visited me in my dreams with that exact snow-white hair when I was a teenager. I could smell the cream in my dream. Something was different in my vision. It seemed incredibly real.

I realized I was not hungry. I was not in pain. I was always hurting in my previous time. My joints constantly pained me. My foot, which I had broken when I was twenty-seven, never healed, and it had never stopped aching. My phantom chest pain, that felt like a boulder was sitting on my chest all the time, wasn't there anymore. I was pain-free for the first time in my life. The constant popping of my ovarian cysts from polycystic ovarian syndrome (PCOS), brought me to my knees every time, I hadn't felt since I had been here on this plane. I looked down at my arms and saw that my keratosis pilaris spots, which never recovered, weren't there. There used to be red spots all over that made me so self-conscious, that I had never worn a tank top in public since I was fifteen. My scars were gone. My body was smooth, fresh, and new. Even the scars from my bout of Pityriasis Rosea were gone. I was finally beautiful.

Chapter 7
The Basis of Earth

The days went on and I grew bigger and bigger. I was not developing at the same rate as on Earth. My mother explained to me that the more my knowledge of this plane expanded, the older I would get. I literally *grew* with *knowledge.*

They started by telling me to forget everything I knew of Earth, humanity, and religion. As well as space and time. There are thousands of solar systems, all having a specific planet that is just far away enough from the sun to sustain *life.*

***

Grandmother chimed in at this point, stating that "Earth *is* heaven and Earth *is* hell. It is a place where the two places coexist to *advance* the people from the previous life. If you can fight off the darkness of Hell and flourish in the peacefulness of Heaven then you get to move on. Some people choose to betray the Heaven around them and focus on Hell. They are the ones that loot and beat others and murder souls just trying to get by to the next life."

"These people *become* the demons on Earth that are feared by everyone. The more demons being made, the more Hell has a hold on the planet. This drives the tornadoes, hurricanes, and massive wildfires taking over half of the United States."

***

The ruthless politicians in office cause more pain for the people trying to live by faith. What is faith? Faith is defined as a complete trust or confidence in someone or something, according to the dictionary. To have faith is not just focusing on *the Lord.* It's believing that everyone should be a good person. To respect and love those around them, even if they do not deserve it. It is protecting the weak and saving the ones who need help from the *Devil* or demons.

God is not a person. It's a being. It's an almighty thought and energy. It's everything that a person should be. On Earth, people believe that there is *one* person that every single one of the over seven billion people on this planet should follow. Seven billion people believing in *one* person. Could you imagine? But, God is not a person. He is everything. A person can *not* be everything. Their physical capabilities do not extend that far. Jesus had flaws. Jesus was said to be the son of God. He was a person to believe in. He is God. God is he. But they focus on him being a son. He had a mother named Mary, who had an immaculate conception. The Catholics believe that Mary should be the one to follow more. So who is to say that Mary isn't the "son" of God and Jesus carried on Mary's beliefs. To explain God hearing *everything* would be to say that he needs all these disciples to listen. This would explain the idea that God can hear and understand all of our thoughts and prayers that we speak in our minds, and on the altar during church...or does it?

Chapter 8
Time and Space

Time wasn't a thing in this world. No one had clocks, no one had dials, you just simply were. No one slept, you know, because we were dead. We just expanded our knowledge, visited with our family, and grew to know them more than we had in the previous life. As we learned lessons, our elders and cousins gained an understanding of the difference between good and evil. How the Earth would be so much more than what it is if people could just filter through the depths of darkness.

Because we never slept and were constantly filling our new brains with knowledge, I grew rapidly. Mind and body. I was finally the size of a *20-year-old* if I was on Earth. I wasn't sure how long I had been dead and I didn't think I would even want to know. The solace that had come from being in this new world was something not many people had ever experienced.

I had had no worries since I had been dead. I didn't have to worry about walking with the thought of *maybe I would get killed.* The worry of getting mugged, or even getting into a car crash. The technology of guns, vehicles, and computers, was nonexistent here.

I was playing with the younger kids that had come here after me, and I had glanced up into the beautiful atmospheric sky. Squinting, I saw something bright and shiny. The sun was reflecting off of the outside of it, making me look away. I also heard and felt something coming from the object, and I could just sense something was there. Something new that I didn't know of yet since rebirthing.

My mother grabbed my hand. She whispered in her head gently to me.

***

"We are not the only ones in this solar system. It was only sci/fi on Earth, but here it happens. Not often, but it does happen," she explained.

***

I asked her if I should be worried, and she affirmed to me *not as of now.* A scarce amount of information was known of their race, but they seemed to understand this was a sacred planet, and they had not tried to intervene with us. They just passed through and didn't concern themselves with us. Our knowledge was great, but not great enough to know of their species. There were some elders who said to be wary, but not scared.

Earth believed they were the only people in the universe, but that was far from the truth. Some people from the military would come out every now and again when their twenty-five years of silence were up, but it had been so long that no one really believed them.

As time went on, the extraterrestrials hung around in our place in space. While they stayed away, it was almost like they slowly worked their way closer to Centauri. Hopefully, they stayed there or even worked their way out of our orbit. Nonetheless, I started to hear whispers from the older and more experienced life forms here, including my great-grandmother. In a world that spoke solely telepathically, it was hard to miss. I heard things like, *they have never stayed around this long, what if they don't leave this time, what if they draw attention to us from Earth.* Just as that thought passed, something very strange happened. Five ships darted past us and one broke away coming in close to our atmosphere where we were standing.

We looked up in awe as this craft hovered about a mountain's height above us with an oscillating sound. Instinctively and habitually I found myself raising my hand at this amazing remarkable ship as if I had some part of a friendship with the entities inside. I felt a sudden glow of warmth fill my body as well as calmness. It was almost as if the craft was communicating with me somehow. As abruptly as the ship appeared, it took off in a flash, and I was left wanting to see it again.

Chapter 9
Welcome Back

The ships continued to come and go around Centauri-b, so we had to just continue with our days. I kept learning as much as I could. One day, my grandmother told me I was ready. I asked her, *ready for what*? She then told me had excelled in my studies of everything I could, and now I was needed elsewhere.

***

"My child, you must go back to Earth. You must go help the people exceed the higher powers' expectations, and help the ones who are trailing behind prosper into the new light," my grandmother explained to me. "I ask one thing of you. Do not dwell on what would have been." I asked her what that meant. "Do not go looking for answers to your questions that I can hear you asking yourself. It will only bring you pain."

***

I felt tired for the first time since I had been here. I couldn't understand. Of all these things I had learned here, why all of a sudden was I flooded with drowsiness? At that moment, my eyelids closed, and I drifted off.

They opened to a place I was so familiar with. It was the last thing I saw before I was sent to Centauri-b. This was the location where I had died. I saw a person riding a bicycle and being cordial. I waved but there was no reply. They did not acknowledge me. I saw a person running, and I stepped in front of them as an experiment. They ran right through me. I realized two things. One, I was still dead. Two, I was sent here to do what my grandmother told me earlier: to help our family.

The first place I was going to go was to my husband. I was going home to see how he was faring in my absence. I still loved him even through the years of abuse, and I was worried about him. I thought of home in my head and all of a sudden, home appeared. I looked through the window to see my husband sitting at the table, alone, drinking and eating dinner. What had he made? The smell of Mongolian Beef wafted through my whole body. It was his favorite meal. I had always made it for his comfort. When he was sad, depressed, hurt, angry, really any emotion, that meal always cheered him up. He would eat excessively until his belly was so swollen, that it looked like it was going to burst.

He seemed sad. I know what I was hoping to find. Maybe I was hoping he would be miserable after I died and would be sorry for the way he treated me. I felt awful for expressing my thoughts that way. Staring through the glass, at this sad man, I heard a door creak open. Out came a redhead from the bathroom. She had a short, black dress on and red high heels. Her hair was curled in a way that it fell off her shoulders and swayed with her swagger. The second she came out of the door, my husband's eyes lit up like the fourth of July. She walked over and caressed his shoulder. Through the door was a bright pink toothbrush sitting on the sink of the bathroom.

At first, I was furious. How could he? Then I thought, maybe it had been a long time since I passed and he had finally healed. I willed myself through the window to look at the walls that showed our life together. There was nothing. I was nowhere. All of our memories were gone from the walls. Vanished. I looked over at the table and the redhead had made herself a salad. No doubt to keep herself starving to look her best for my husband.

***

"I had no idea my dead wife was keeping me from the most beautiful woman I have ever seen. I'm glad she's gone. I wish I would've found you six months sooner, so I could've told her sayonara when she was still alive," he said as he wrapped his arms around her waist.

***

I heard my grandmother's voice in my head telling me I shouldn't have looked for the answers to my questions because it would only bring me to hurt. I vowed to stay true to that now. I was no longer an earthling. I was a spirit dweller and here for a purpose. That purpose was not to make myself sad. I willed the lights to flicker so I could just let him know I was there and could see what he was doing. I didn't know if it would work or not but I tried. Just then, the light above the table popped. Both of them stood up quickly. They sat back down after it came back on.

***

"It was probably just the wind," he stated.

"What if it was your dead wife haunting us?" she snickered.

***

From that comment, I blew the breaker and made all of the lights go out. I wasn't necessarily angry anymore, it was more so to let him know that I know the man he had become, and most likely had always been. I left them in the dark to continue my quest.

Chapter 10
Expedition News

As I walked down the road, I tried to consider who I could help in my family. I thought of all the ones who were on the wrong path that I'd wished I could be of assistance to before. My oldest brother left the family and moved away with no contact. I had heard things previously of him just surviving, not living, on a river in Montana. My other brother had been a prior service member but could not get work after he got out. There were many cousins who strayed away from the path of righteousness due to the way we were all raised. Where should I even start? How do I start? My grandmother had come to me in a dream, so maybe I could infiltrate their minds at night without seeming suspicious and giving myself away.

I decided to start with a cousin who had a very rough start in life. She was adopted into the family from a mother and father who were drug addicts and couldn't care for themselves let alone an innocent baby. She became of age and she whored herself out to older men, enveloped herself in pot, and treated herself like she was nothing. I had always wanted to just come up to her and shake her and say, *stop doing this to yourself. You're so much more than this. Take what you have been given and show your biological family that you are so much more than them.*

That night, I willed my energy into her dreams.

***

"Freesia, what are you doing here? Oh wait, I must be dreaming," she said to me.

"No Daffney, it's me. The real me. I need you to know something," I explained to her.

"This is crazy, I must be tripping on those 'shrooms I took earlier," she replied.

***

This wasn't working. I didn't know why I thought my first attempt would be successful. You couldn't just change someone in a few minutes. How could I do this in the short time I had in this delusion?

***

"I know this sounds crazy, Daff, but you have to listen to me. Earth is heaven and hell combined. In order to move on to the next life, you have to make better choices. The new world is so much better than this one. But you can't get there by sinning your way through life." I tried explaining the best I could, but how do you explain bliss?

"This is weird and uncomfortable. I need to stop doing so many drugs," she jested to herself.

***

And with that, she woke up, and I was left in the dark. I had failed my first task. I assumed not everyone would be successful on their first time back on Earth, but I just felt like the failure that I was before I had died. I was not the person for this job. Daffney turned on the television, so I decided to just sit there and soak in my uselessness.

As she was watching a television show I had watched many times when I was alive, a special news update popped on the channel. Daff tried to turn to the next channel because obviously, she didn't enjoy news bulletins. Every single channel ended up having a special news update.

***

"To the United States of America," the IPAWS showed up on the television. It was an integrated public alert & warning system.

"The National Aeronautics and Space Administration has alerted the President that multiple unidentified flying objects have been spotted outside the solar system near a planet we all have come to know as Centauri-b. Due to the distance away from our planet, we have not been able to see exactly what is on the planet, but we do know that UFOs have been spotted skittering around the world. We are not aware of our life being in imminent danger."

***

No, this couldn't be true. The Earth itself and the politicians could not know of our world. It would destroy our sacred space. The governments would try to politicize and destroy our lands because it was different, and *not* what anyone else believed. Earth hated things that were different. The aliens that were hovering over Centauri-b were about to give up our position and ruin everything that was made for us in the next life. I had to warn my grandmother and the elders.

Chapter 11
Earth to Centauri, Hello?

I thought I could just will my way back home. Apparently, that was *not* how this works. I tried everything. Jumping through walls, yelling, praying, I even went as far as forcing my energy into the ley lines of the world. Nothing worked. After much energy was wasted, I was exhausted. What could I do now?

I got an idea. Since I couldn't seem to get back to Centauri to warn everyone, maybe I could go to NASA and see just what all they knew. Perhaps it wasn't something to worry about.

I closed my eyes and thought of Washington D.C. It was a place I had not visited before. I imagined the big blue circle, with the white orbit and red chevron. The stars encircling the sphere that is supposed to represent the planet and the big white letters that spelled out its acronym. I imagined space crafts and astronauts, computers and technology the people of Earth had rarely seen. The massive telescope that spotted the flying ships. All of these items would surely send me to where I wanted to go, despite not knowing where it was actually located.

I was still so new to this traveling thing, but it was so important for me to get there. As I slowly opened my eyes, I saw right before me the giant blue circle I had imagined in my mind. I made it here at least. Now to figure out who knew the most about the ships.

I walked through more than one hundred walls and I was so turned around. A lost ghost, how funny. I decided to sit down on the bench beside me and wait until I came up with another plan. Or I could just yell so loud, Grandmother could hear. I leaned my head against the wall and closed my eyes.

***

"Sir, another ship has appeared," stated a man walking by on his telephone. "I'll meet you over there." He ran off down the hall. I followed.

***

The distinct smell of cigar smoke floated through the air when the General walked in with a confident demeanor and motivated personality. He kept to the traditional airs of his position as a high-ranking military officer. Those around him were bustling about in nervousness and/or completely unaware of his prestige as they held one of their own high-minded genius. Narcissism was definitely running on overload in this tense yet very controlled chaos of a control room.

***

"Three ships from an alien race have shown up around Centauri-b. We believe something of significance is there that we cannot see. We must find a way to get closer to the end of this solar system. Does anyone, *anyone* have any ideas?" One man said.

"We could take the James Webb Space Telescope as far through space as we can to the edge of the solar system towards Centauri-b," another man suggested.

***

I couldn't let them take that telescope out there. It would surely see the planet and who knew if it'd see through the mask of the atmosphere. To devise a plan, I thought of any of my family members that may be able to help. We didn't have the best bloodline. We didn't have any engineers, doctors, or anything of significance. We were all basically farmers and store employees. No one would believe someone like us. Especially not someone from NASA.

I had an idea. I closed my eyes and willed myself to one of my farming cousin's houses. Cousin Cybal was a widow. She lost her husband a few years back and was left to tend her farm by herself. She had no kids due to developing cervical cancer in her 20s and having all of her reproductive organs removed. I thought maybe she would be the perfect person to help.

When I appeared at her home, Cybal was outside tending her garden. She was an elderly lady, around 84 years old. She had bright silver hair that used to be blonde, and she was skinny like a stick.

Her skin was falling off of her bones. I hadn't really talked to her ever when I was alive so I wasn't sure of her story. I would wait here and lurk, for lack of a better term, until she went to sleep. I watched her water her garden, pick off dead leaves and stems, and pull a few weeds. She did everything with a sense that she had all the time in the world. I guess that was what happens when you get to a certain age. You were basically waiting to die and not in a rush to do anything.

I watched her walk into her home after being outside for hours. She went to her kitchen sink and washed her hands. She took her scrub brush and cleaned daintily under her fingernails, taking care that each nail was thoroughly scrubbed and had no filth underneath. Then she took a washcloth and carefully washed all the skin up to her elbow. She must have scrubbed too hard as blood began to trickle down her arm. With every swipe, more blood saturated her pale skin red. Cybal leaned over to her medicine cabinet and pulled out a large bandaid. She pressed it to her wound, but somehow all of the blood just engorged it. She must be on a blood thinner regimen.

With her arm still leaking, she walked over to her stove to make dinner. Cybal grabbed a handful of dry noodles and a stick of butter. Next, she grabbed a small jar of green beans, no doubt from her garden. She placed everything in a pot and turned the knobs to cook. Her small arms grabbed a plate from her cupboard. She proceeded to grab a fork and placed it on a sunflower napkin. I glanced at her wound and still, it bled. She ignored it like it had happened millions of times.

Her face was starting to turn white. All the color on her face perished. I could feel her slipping away. She must be losing too much blood for her small, frail body to keep up with. No phone calls were made. I wondered if she was to get to a certain point if I would be able to show myself. This might be a better way than to meet her in her dreams. My cousin made herself a plate and sat down at the table. One bite...two bites...three bites...I willed myself to show up at that kitchen table. She looked up.

Chapter 11
Save the World, Cybal

Cybal looked up nonchalantly. It apparently wasn't weird to her that a stranger was sitting across from her that hadn't been there two seconds before.

***

"Would you like a plate of food, child?" she asked me without pause.

"Do you know who I am?" I questioned.

"You're obviously a spirit because no one ever visits me. I have been alone for years on this property," she replied. "My arm won't stop bleeding. Are you here to stop it?"

***

She seemed so innocent. She was the perfect person for Centauri-b.

***

"Tell me about yourself, Cybal," I asked her sweetly.

***

She told me about growing up in the Great Depression out in Kansas. How her family had nothing but cows to keep them alive. Their only money came from the meat and milk. Once the depression was at its worst, they had no cash. No funds meant they couldn't feed the cattle. There was no rain to make the grass grow, and that was their last hope for the animals to flourish. Half her immediate family died from starvation. The other half died from the tornados and dust storms that wrecked the plains.

She had a husband and her two sisters lived with them. They got killed from the amount of dust that filled their lungs during a dust storm. They were trying to get the cattle into the barn before it fell to its knees. She was unable to go outside and call for them because she was making dinner. There wasn't a window in front of her stove. She has beaten herself up ever since, thinking that maybe if she would have seen the storm coming, she could have saved them.

Cybal sold the farm and moved to Ohio after that. She never remarried. She bought a small house with a little bit of land in the middle of nowhere, away from corn fields or people. Her new property was surrounded by forest. She was so distraught from her family that she became a recluse. Her garden was her safe house.

***

"I'm so sorry you had to go through all of that, Cybal," I said through my tears.

"Don't be sorry. It's just the way God wanted my life to go. Perhaps I have a bigger reason to be here and not them.

"Your arm is bleeding more." I glanced down at her frailness.

"I'm feeling quite weak, I think I am going to go lay down now," she replied quietly.

***

She was fading away. I had to tell her. She seemed very open-minded. I might as well just come out and say it.

***

"Cybal, I need you to listen to me very carefully, and I need you to stay awake until I'm done. Can you do that?" I smiled at her through worried eyes, and she nodded back.

"I died six months ago. I am your cousin, Freesia. I awoke in a world that is nothing like this one. It's called Centauri-b. It holds the sweetest souls that have lived on this Earth. Earth unfortunately is a test for the beyond. It is Heaven *and* Hell."

"Centauri-b, I have heard of that before. On the news? Yes, that's right, on the news. Aliens? You are an alien?" she rebutted.

"No, no, the aliens are beings from the neighboring solar system. They are floating around Centauri, and are making people look towards the skies more. I am serious when I say they *cannot* know about Centauri. They cannot know what happens after death. It would completely destroy everyone's religion and knowledge of everything they have ever known. It would be disastrous. I'm unable to reach Centauri-b because my job is here on Earth. You, Cybal, must tell the elders what is happening. Tell them they are sending the telescope out in space to get closer to the aliens and closer to the new world. Can you do that?" I pleaded with her.

***

She caressed my hand and laid it on her chest. I felt her heartbeat slow to a stop. She died with a smile on her face. All I could do was hope...

Chapter 12
Today's Forecast: Expect Extraterrestrials?

What could I do while I waited for word from Centauri-b? Would I even get a response from them? I could go buzz around NASA and see if they are saying anything. I also came back to this planet for a reason. Should I help people like I am supposed to? Such a big decision. I wondered if I could find another being like me. This whole time I've been here, I haven't seen or heard anyone. I couldn't be the only one who has this *job*. A thought provoked my mind.

How was Cybal going to be found? No one was missing her. She had no friends and no family left. I wondered if it would be wrong of me to interfere. I really was not told any rules I had to follow. If Cybal ended up in Centauri like I had hoped she would, I'm sure she would want a proper burial, and not be left alone or forgotten. I moved into the local town and looked around for the police station. I flowed inside and waited until the officer walked away. I picked up a pen and wrote down Cybal's address and the words *help me* on the desk, then left the building.

I would branch out until I heard something, whether from the other world or from here on the news. A month on Earth had gone by since my encounter with Cybal, and I was able to sway some people in my family to make better decisions on this planet. Some were drug addicts, some were thieves, and others just didn't know their heads from their buttocks. A lot of them just ignored me and assumed they were completely dreaming. I didn't know why I was sent here because I really hadn't talked to anyone before I died, nor had I any family that I really spoke with. Those seeing me in their dreams didn't even know that I was dead half the time.

The day had been like every other day, with no one listening. They were pushing me off and telling me I was fake. One person had the news on, though. It was the local weather channel talking about the storm rolling in. There has been an enormous amount of weird weather lately all across the world. Most just chalked it up to El Niño, otherwise known as a warming of the ocean surface. As they were doing interviews with random strangers as they liked to do, one mentioned that they thought the incredulous weather was being constructed by the aliens surrounding Centauri-b. They cut him off as soon as he mentioned that planet. Typical for people to just assume others with differing opinions are conspiracists.

The news promptly went to sports. The sportscaster was laughing and talking about how that guy needed to go outside for some fresh air to clear his mind. I knew better. Great-grandma had told me back on Centauri to be aware of the ships at all times. They didn't know if they were bad but they definitely didn't believe they were good. I snapped back from my thoughts as a news bulletin sounded. *Just in, NASA has readied the James Webb Telescope enough to be able to send it into space to get a closer look at the unidentified floating objects in space. The launch will be happening this evening at 5 p.m. eastern time. Back to your local programming.* Shoot. I had to get to the building before they launched. I willed my way to D.C.

Everyone was running around the campus like lab rats. Hundreds of people were gathered around the launch site. The chattering of the mass sounded like a Lynyrd Skynyrd concert as Ronnie Van Zant walked on stage. Some of the workers were putting the finishing touches on the primary mirrors. These parts were made to withstand a small amount of debris and micrometeoroids, and according to scientists, this should be enough. This would be the first time this telescope had been launched into space. They weren't sure if it would survive the trek to the edge of the solar system, but they were willing to risk the millions of dollars they'd spent on this piece of technology to save the planet that they believed was in peril.

Later, a voice came on over the loudspeaker that stated: *it is now 4:37 p.m. eastern time. Approximately 23 minutes until launch. Please back away from the platform.*

When this all started, I had made a firm decision to will myself into the room I was in to see if there was any headway before the launch. Some guy was talking in front of all of the employees in the room. It was definitely in Chinese. The guy standing beside him was presumably the translator. He was trying to keep up with the Chinese guy talking quickly. I didn't think he could keep up because his English translation was very broken. What I did hear was that without China's involvement, it would take the telescope over 19,000 years to get to Centauri-b. They needed China's aid to get there faster. He wouldn't say how unless they allowed them to intervene before the rocket blasted off.

The Americans were flabbergasted. There was no way they wanted China's help. That would mean China would be saving the world and not the United States. Just then, a massive whiteboard came protruding out of the ceiling and let itself down to the floor. A picture of a phone appeared. The whole room went silent. The soldiers that were around for what I believe was security stood at attention and raised their arms in a salute. The president appeared on the screen. The translator looked like he was going to pass out. His skin went pale, sweat cascaded down his face, and his knees buckled.

The back and forth bantering between the President and the Chinese man and the translator went on for quite a few minutes. The launch time was dwindling to almost minutes now. Just then, the Chinese man bowed and jogged out of the room. The President agreed that they would need China's help. It turned out, that China was on the verge of developing ways for rockets to travel at lightspeed, turning the voyage from a 19,000-year mission to a 4-year mission. At least I had time to work out a way to get back to Centauri to warn them if Cybal hadn't made it.

The launch was pushed to the next day as China installed their new light speed engineering into the rocket. Putting trust into a design that hadn't been tested on an actual rocket had everyone on edge. At 4 p.m. the next day, a loud siren started up. It was the launch sequence. I glanced out of the window with worried eyes as the rocket started smoking and fire blasted out of the engines. *We have lift off.*

Chapter 13
To the Edge of the Galaxy, and Beyond

The weeks after the telescope launched into space, there was constant chatter. All over the news, reporters were following the trek to Centauri-b. They wrote and spoke of literally every asteroid the telescope passed. Every star they came across. At one point, the telescope even sent pictures of a traveling black hole the world didn't know about yet. They knew there was already one black hole in the middle of the universe, but this random black hole that popped up wherever it wanted with no rhyme or reason was big news. The stationary hole was named *MOA-11-191*. Who knew what the moving black hole would do in the coming months?

As the rocket carrying the telescope traveled to its destination, the black hole that moved began to follow. No matter which course the telescope took, the black hole would pop up right in its line of movement. They would have to change course as soon as it appeared so that the hole did not suck up the rocket and destroy millions of dollars of equipment. The news had a special report that NASA was looking for experienced engineers around the globe so that the rocket could be watched 24 hours a day, 7 days a week. All of the engineers who were working at the building had done everything in their power to come up with a system that would alert the workers *before* the black hole would appear. Everything they tried, failed. There was just no way to determine why or when that hole would show itself.

While the rocket got deeper into space, it was harder to track when the black hole appeared. The farther away from the sun and the stars, where the light bent toward the hole, was diminishing. A black hole is basically invisible unless there is a light source. The rocket was not equipped with any high-power lighting due to the quickness of which it was thrown into space. No one was prepared for a wandering black hole to follow.

The black hole flooded the news agencies and the long name and numbers got to be too much to continually say, so it became known as *The Barren.* Barren meant a place bleak, and lifeless, and that is exactly what they thought this hole was. Conspiracy theorists began to correlate the path of The Barren with the path to the aliens and a theory emerged. What if The Barren was actually the aliens' way to jump through space to get closer to the Earth? All of the synapses in my mind started bursting with energy. The aliens.

Had my plan to have Cybal warn Centauri actually worked? If it did, how would the aliens know? So much unknown, and terror. Were they good guys? Bad guys? Were they even *science fiction* aliens? Or just creatures from that universe, and the people of Earth were the aliens to them. I could only hope they were trying to help keep Centauri-b safe and sacred. The amount of knowledge I acquired after death was so extreme, that I could not place why I couldn't figure out who these extraterrestrials were. I guessed the game of wait and see would continue.

After weeks and months of the news covering The Barren, they sort of trickled off into other news. There was still quite a long time until the telescope reached the edge of our galaxy. It's funny, that even in times of devastation, the world gets bored of the same old news. They wanted to hear more about the killings, murders, and protests. The devil loves the media, and its demons follow the masses.

Chapter 14
Mission: Avoid the Space Trash

As the rocket continued to dart between The Barren, debris started coming out of the hole. At first, it was small space debris, minuscule asteroids that orbit the planets naturally. The mirrors on the rocket were built to withstand these items because the engineers knew of their existence. They knew there were broken satellites and *all-around space trash* circling the orbits. The rocket was a good way away from any of the planets in the galaxy so they were not sure why it was coming through the black hole. There was an eerie pattern between the intervals that the space junk came out of The Barren, though.

What the engineers didn't take into account when they okayed China to install the light-speed technology, was the change of force that even the smallest piece of space debris would affect the rocket. A paint chip, at that velocity, could go right through the plating of the rocket because of physics. I learned this from my awakening of knowledge after my death. This could be used to the advantage of saving Centauri-b due to the fact that no one was taking that into account.

The debris was beginning to pick up after every interval and it was hard for the engineers, who were watching it, to miss them. A pebble here and rock there started to hit the mirrors. The more pieces that hit, the more the mirrors cracked. There was nothing anyone could do, besides trying to miss them, but watch and wait. They tried to change course to throw off The Barren, but somehow The Barren always knew where they were going. The conspiracy of it being the aliens started to become more realistic.

As the days and weeks continued on the journey to Centauri-b, the mass of the items that shot out of the hole were becoming larger and more defined. Subsequently, debris from around Earth started dwindling. More and more *trash* that was orbiting the planet was disappearing. Unexpectedly, parts from the Sputnik-1 came crashing out of The Barren. How did that get there? How was any of this getting there? Even so, was this helping their future? Was it helping our future? Getting rid of space junk around the Earth meant less chance of collision and less chance of destroying the earth and satellites.

The rocket finally made its way to the edge of the solar system. A place where no one had been before. Pictures started appearing from the telescope. A whole new space was appearing before Earth's optics. They were able to start mapping out the new expanse firsthand. New planets, new stars, new everything. NASA had some sort of idea from 4 light-years away, but in the amount of time it took the pictures to get to the Earth originally, it was old news. It was like an episode of Star Trek to them. The engineers took this terrible scenario and started using it for good. To have an up-close and personal look at a new space in space.

Earth's skies began to darken, leaving a beautiful night sky in the wake of the space debris getting moved. The more space debris, the more objects that give off light from the sun, which means brighter night skies. Scintillating night skies drain the darkness of the beautiful stars that are in the great void. People were able to glance at planets that otherwise couldn't be seen only on certain days of the year when they were closest to Earth. More people were looking toward the skies instead of at their enemies. To take a moment and see something as beautiful as a sky filled with stars, had slowed the amount of crime even to the smallest degree.

Huge chunks of space trash started jolting out of The Barren. One chunk slammed into the right-side mirror. It shattered into a million pieces and floated off into space. Another chunk soared into the left side mirror and broke that one also. The computers at NASA activated red warning signals all over. The overhead machine showing the schematics of the rocket conveyed the damage to the ship.

WARNING! WARNING! WARNING! INCOMING!

Pluto emerged from The Barren. If no one thought Pluto wasn't big enough to be a planet, they did now. It plowed into the rocket. The computer screens back on Earth went black. The feed was completely offline. The building was extensively quiet. Nobody knew what had happened. How in the world did Pluto come through the black hole? While everyone was in awe and silence, one team member who was sitting at the screen that showed the solar system dropped his coffee mug and it fractured into pieces. All eyes were on him when he lifted his finger to the screen in front of him. The Barren appeared in our solar system just outside of Neptune's orbit.

Did they panic? Did they scream? A few had fainted. They were convinced that The Barren was going to do some more damage to the planets. As fast as Pluto shot through The Barren into the rocket carrying the telescope to seek out the aliens, Pluto once again came spinning out of the black hole into its rightful place in the solar system unscathed. The Barren then flashed in a sequence that was later found to be morse code for *stop looking goodbye.* The Barren disappeared into the vast plain of nothingness that is space.

Chapter 15
Post-Pluto

As people inside the NASA headquarters picked their jaws off of the ground, no one broke the silence of the building. You could hear a feather wisp in the breeze of a fan. Never in their history had they seen such a phenomenon. No one in the world had experienced what just happened except the people in that building. Pluto disappeared and returned so quickly, it was like a blip in the system and would have been a fantasy if it had not been recorded. The President was brought up to speed on what transpired, and he stated not to tell anyone yet. The President and the Chinese leaders ordered the phones at all NASA buildings to be turned off.

The following week no one spoke of the incident. Everyone just stared at the same screen that showed our solar system with *all* planets in alignment where they should be. Space ships that had been near Centauri were no longer there. They disappeared the second Pluto was thrown back into its spot in the system. Every person that entered or left the building from that day, had to sign a non-disclosure agreement. If they mentioned anything whatsoever about what happened, the government would be the ones to sue them and it would destroy them.

The President finally issued a statement that was very blanketed. He decided it wouldn't have been feasible. Knowing the citizens of the United States, there could even have been a massive uproar in protest that they weren't told what was going on.

***

The President addressed the nation: "Citizens of the United States, I realize you must be very intrigued by what has been going on in space, but do not fret. The extra-terrestrial ships that were surrounding the exo-planet Centauri-b have disappeared. There is no longer a threat to planet Earth."

***

The phones were then engaged, at which point, they started ringing off the hooks. Reporters from all over wanted to know where the ships had disappeared to. They also continually asked why they had been unable to reach any of the NASA buildings in the last week. The phone operators tried to explain that the phone company was doing work on all of the buildings at the same time and no one was reachable until they finished correcting the lines.

This of course caused an exorbitant amount of controversy. The government tracked the internet for any signs that anyone was close to figuring out what happened. Not many people got it correct since it was so quick of an incident. For the very few that did, the government deleted it from all of the websites. While this may have been causing for concern to the person, it was to keep the world safe another day.

I had been watching this all play out and I was just in awe at the amount the government went to hide this. It made me wonder even more about what they had been hiding all of these years. We have had so many conspiracy theories that the officials tried to cover up. Especially J.F.K.'s death. To this day no one actually knows the details of the truth.

This huge part of history would go down as a non-combatant spaceship that was here and then disappeared, and that was it.

Chapter 16
Recalled

A tingling sensation began shooting through my whole body. It was a familiar feeling. I remember this from the moment I slammed into the wall divider. I closed my eyes and let my being succumb to the feeling. The sensation got stronger and stronger. I didn't know how long it had been happening. It subsided into me not feeling anything at all. I could smell colors. I opened my eyes to see the beautiful world of Centauri-b. The mass of people that had been there when I left, were all standing in front of me. A hoard of thank yous and great jobs came roaring into my mind.

Cybal and my great-grandmother emerged from the crowd of people. They wrapped their arms around me and kissed my cheeks. I felt the warmth of unconditional love being passed through my body.

***

"It's so good to see you here, Cybal," I thought to her.

"And to you, my child," she answered back.

***

I wondered in my head if anyone had known where the black hole had come from. Immediately, they grabbed my hand and led me into an area that had hundreds of chairs in a circle. My grandmother ushered me into a chair beside my mother and Cybal. She told me the story of how Cybal was born into this new world. She had to learn just like everyone else did on this plane. She was born a baby and grew at a pace somewhat slower than I had when I came to Centauri. Because she had been on Earth for much longer than I had, it was a more time-consuming affair.

When Cybal was knowledgeable enough to know what was going on in the new world and new way of life, she was finally able to remember what had gone on right before her death. When Cybal was done explaining to the elders what was happening, the extra-terrestrial ships that had been surrounding Centauri-b this whole time came into the atmosphere. A bright light shined out of the door that opened and leveled with the ground but no one could see anything. They could tell someone or something was in the middle of the scorching light.

A voice came through everyone's minds. It was deep and pronounced. It was exceptionally stoic and yet loving. The voice told everyone that the ships were going to help keep the rocket away from Centauri-b. It turned out that the ships were hovering to protect them, as they knew something was going to happen to the spiritual world in the near future. The being went on to describe that even if they hadn't shown themselves as they did, Earth was so close to figuring out that the cloak on Centauri was a facade, and they would have come this way anyway. Putting the world in the predicament it did, the aliens or beings would be able to be in the vicinity to save them.

***

"Centauri is a plane of beauty and peace. No one should ever know about this until they have met their end on Earth. We must keep you safe. The very existence of space, time, and future depends on you and all of these *angels* that go back to fix the demons' work. Continue your practices. Spread love and joy. Defeat the darkness."

***

With that, the door to the ship closed, the light disappeared, and all of the ships surrounding Centauri vanished into the vacuum of space.

The elders congregated together and spoke to one another at a frequency that no one else on the planet could hear. They all came to the conclusion that the destiny of Centauri-b was in the hands of this being. Furthermore, it came with a presence so familiar, that it may or may not have been God himself. I don't think we will ever know just who it was. All we know is, that being saved our world and we must cherish what we have.

My grandmother explained to me that everyone who *can* and is *ready* to go change the Earth will. Everyone must do all they can to fix what is broken so that more and more people will see the light. Getting rid of the evils of the world will brighten the future of Heaven for all of those that come after.

My mother and grandmother gave me a hug.

***

"Go help the ones who need you back on Earth. We will be awaiting your return, "my grandmother declared.

***

What boggled my mind was the fact that I had seen no other spirit like me during my time on Earth. My mother laughed, and the tingling sensation engulfed my body once again. I was back on Earth in my spirit form. Immediately I saw millions of entities following the living around. Perhaps, my purpose was actually to save the world on my own...

Synopsis

Freesia's life had always been monotonous. Between failed relationships and a verbally abusive husband, she thought her life was going to go nowhere.

One day, time stopped for her during a crash on her way to her bland 9-5 job...

A new world opened up to her. Was it a dream? No, it was Centauri-b.

A secret world, an immaculate view. Aliens? NASA? She is going to have to find a way to save a place that is so unknown, that Russia doesn't even know about it.

Will she be able to overcome her new challenges? With the help of her deceased family, and the living, the hurdles she will jump over will leave you windless.

Suspense, drama, and a little bit of sci/fi, this story will take you on a whole new adventure into a world of Heaven and Hell. Maybe, it is Earth.

About the Author

I am a stay-at-home mother of four children. I just published my first book Deerly beloved on May 17th, 2022. Exodus-b is my second book. My next upcoming novel is The Cycle of Unsound Town.

I enjoy crafting, painting, gardening, reading, and writing.

I grow my own salsa-makings. I currently have 95 pepper plants, 23 tomato plants, 24 cucumber plants, romaine, and all kinds of herbs planted. I make on average 200 to 300 jars of salsa every year from medium all the way to insanely hot.

I hand paint terra cotta pots in my free time. I make character faces and animals. They all have different personalities and no two are the same.

My living room is a library. I love collecting books. Nothing quite like it! Every inch of my walls are covered in packed bookshelves that don't have furniture on them. My children love reading also and I am always buying new books to fill shelves.

I plan to continue to write and self-publish my books so my children can be proud of me!

www.ingramcontent.com/pod-product-compliance
Lightning Source LLC
Chambersburg PA
CBHW030415310726
48979CB00002B/426

* 9 7 9 8 9 8 6 6 0 5 9 0 6 *